Bugs Bunny's™
Carrot Machine

By Clark Carlisle

Illustrated by Anthony Strobl and Bob Totten

A GOLDEN BOOK • NEW YORK

Western Publishing Company, Inc., Racine, Wisconsin 53404

ISBN: 0-307-00111-3   MCMXCII

One day Bugs Bunny came running out of a secondhand bookshop in great excitement. He bumped into Elmer Fudd.

"Whoa, wabbit!" Elmer cried. "What's the wush?"

"Look what I found in an old magazine!" Bugs replied. "The plans for a carrot-making machine! Want to help me build one?"

Elmer looked at the plans. "I'll be glad to," he said, "if it'll keep you out of my garden! According to these plans, all we need to build your machine are some pieces of junk."

"Forward, then . . . to the town trash heap!" cried Bugs. Dreams of fresh, crisp, golden carrots filled his head. "I'll be rich!" he gloated. "With a carrot machine, I'll never be hungry again!"

At the city dump, Bugs and Elmer found an old boiler. They filled it with junk—plumbing pipes, auto parts, old clothes, broken bottles, rusty nails—and carried it to Elmer's backyard. There, following the plans, they set to work building the carrot machine.

Soon it was finished. It had a spout in front, a funnel on top, a red underwear button in back, and pipes sticking out of it every which way.

"You think this thing will make carrots?" asked Elmer doubtfully.

"We followed the plans," said Bugs. "Let's try it out!"

Bugs pushed the red button on the back of the machine.
Nothing happened.

"See?" Elmer said. "The cwazy thing doesn't work. It
says here," he said, looking at the plans, "that we have
to put in some ingwedients."

Bugs read the instructions himself. *To operate machine, fill up with anything handy and push button. Don't overload.* Bugs immediately began to throw some of their leftover junk into the funnel on top of the carrot machine. Elmer helped him.

"Now!" cried Bugs. "Let's see what happens." He pushed the red button again.

Zap!—the carrot machine suddenly came to life! It began to sputter and smoke. Then, with a dry coughing sound, it blew a small, square, green object out of its spout and onto the ground.

Bugs picked it up. "Some carrot!" he said. "Wrong shape and wrong color!"

"How does it taste, though?" Elmer asked. "That's what weally counts."

Bugs nibbled at the square, green carrot. "Hey!" he cried in surprise. "It's not half bad, Elmer! See what you think."

Elmer took a bite. "I think it's a little tough, Bugs. We ought to season it so it's softer."

Bugs looked around and found a moth-eaten sofa pillow. "Here's something pretty soft," he said. He stuffed the pillow down the funnel and pushed the button.

Another small, square, green carrot came out of the spout. Bugs tasted it.

"Perfect!" he shouted. "Delicious!" Then he frowned. "But who ever heard of eating square, green carrots? I'd be laughed at by every rabbit in town!" He scratched one ear. "I need something pointed," he said, and he tossed three rusty iron spikes into the machine.

This time the machine spit out a carrot that was still green and still small—but it was pointed at one end, just like a real carrot!

Bugs knew the secret now. "Find something orange-colored!" he cried. "That ought to do it."

Elmer hunted around until he found a broken mar-
malade jar with an orange label on it. He tossed it into
the machine. "Now twy it," he said.

Bugs pushed the button. This time the carrot was just perfect. It had the right color, the right shape, and the right taste.

But Bugs still wasn't satisfied. "I want 'em bigger!" he said. "These little bitty carrots hardly make half a mouthful!" He gathered up everything else in their heap of trash and threw it all into the machine. "Now we'll get some decent-sized carrots," he said.

The carrot machine shook and shuddered and smoked. It ground and coughed and sputtered. But no carrot came out of its spout. And then, all of a sudden and with a dreadful bang, the carrot machine exploded into hundreds of pieces! One piece hit Bugs and knocked him head over heels.

"Now you've done it, you gweedy wabbit!" Elmer scolded him. "You've overloaded the machine. It's completely wuined!"

"Cheer up, Doc. We'll make another," said Bugs, picking himself up. "Where'd I put those plans?"

"You thwew them into the machine with evewything else," Elmer said. "So there'll be no more carrot machines for you, you cwazy wabbit! I hope this has taught you a lesson."

"Oh, it sure has, Doc!" Bugs grinned at his friend. "Just look at what's left of our beautiful carrot machine. It's pointing the way to something even better."

Elmer stared down at the pieces of junk. They had fallen to the ground in the shape of an arrow.

"You wascally wabbit, you!" Elmer shouted. "Don't you dare!"

For, sure enough, the arrow pointed straight to Elmer's prized carrot patch!